Fruits

HEALTHY ME

Published by Smart Apple Media
1980 Lookout Drive, North Mankato, Minnesota 56003

PHOTOGRAPHS BY Richard Cummins, Tom Stack & Associates (Milton Rand, Inga Spence,
Greg Vaughn), Unicorn Stock Photos (Joel Dexter, James L. Fly, Ron P. Jaffe, Marie Mills,
Gary Randall, Aneal E. Vohra, Lee Watson)
DESIGN BY Evansday Design

Library of Congress Cataloging-in-Publication Data
Kalz, Jill.
Fruits / by Jill Kalz.
p. cm. — (Healthy me)
Summary: Describes different kinds of fruits and their importance in a healthy diet.
Includes bibliographical references.
ISBN 1-58340-299-3
1. Fruit—Juvenile literature. [1. Fruit. 2. Nutrition.] I. Title.

TX558.F7 K35 2003
641.3´4—dc21   2002030623

First Edition

9 8 7 6 5 4 3 2 1

Fruits

Trees, Bushes, and Vines

Fruits grow almost everywhere. Orange trees love warm, sunny places. Banana plants grow where it is hot and wet. Grape **vines** like a little sun and a little rain.

Fruit trees, bushes, and vines grow flowers first. After the flowers die, fruits grow. A fruit is the part of a plant that holds seeds. Peaches have one big seed. Apples have many little seeds. Each seed could grow into a new plant.

One big seed grows inside every peach.

< Grapes grow in bunches on vines.

Farmers pick most fruits when they are **ripe.** They use their hands or machines. Then the fruits are loaded onto trucks, ships, or airplanes and sent to stores.

Fruit tree farms are called orchards.
Apples, cherries, and peaches
grow in orchards.

The small seeds in apples, oranges,
and other fruits are called pips.

A Rainbow of Fruits

Fruits can be any color. They can be red like cherries. Yellow like bananas or lemons. Orange like peaches. Green like grapes or limes. Blue like blueberries. Or purple like plums.

Some fruits have thick skins. Oranges and bananas have thick skins. You must **peel** them before you eat them. Other fruits have thin skins. You can eat apples, grapes, and cherries without peeling them.

Many fruits have thin skins you can eat. ︿

‹ Blueberries are named for their color.

Every fruit tastes different. Some are sweet. Some are sour. Apples crunch. Watermelon is juicy. Raisins are chewy.

Jellies and jams are made from fruits. Juices are made from crushed apples, oranges, or other fruits. Wine is a grown-up's drink made from crushed grapes.

Wine is often kept in wooden barrels. ⌃

< Watermelons are hard outside and juicy inside.

The Good Stuff

Fruits have important **vitamins** that everybody needs. Vitamin C helps heal cuts and bruises. It fights colds. And it helps keep teeth healthy. Oranges have a lot of vitamin C. So do strawberries.

Fruits also have vitamin A and fiber. Vitamin A keeps hair, skin, and eyes healthy. Fiber helps move food through your body.

Fruits help keep your body healthy. ∧

< Strawberries are full of vitamin C.

Eating fresh fruits is the best way to get these vitamins. Most fruit juice is good, too. But some juices and canned fruits have sugar added. Too much sugar can be bad for you.

Apples and bananas are the two most popular fruits eaten in the United States.

⌄

Banana bunches grow in short rows called hands. Each banana is called a finger.

Eating Right

All foods belong to one of five food groups. Fruits belong to the fruits group. Foods made from milk belong to the dairy group. There are also groups for vegetables, meats, and grains.

Your body needs a lot of fruit. Doctors say you

should eat two to four helpings of fruit each day.

A helping may be one apple. A handful of raisins.

Or a small glass of orange juice.

A handful of cherries makes a good snack. ⌃

⟨ Your body needs all kinds of foods.

It is important to eat foods from all of the food groups. Each group has things your body needs. Fruits are sweet treats that are also good for you!

Raisins are dried grapes. About half of the world's raisins come from California.

Tomatoes belong to the fruits group. But many people use them as vegetables.

Fruit Shake

This drink is made from two food groups. Bananas and strawberries belong to the fruits group. Milk and ice cream belong to the dairy group.

WHAT YOU NEED

A banana
Three strawberries
One cup (240 ml) milk
Two scoops vanilla ice cream
An electric blender

WHAT YOU DO

1. Peel the banana.
2. Wash the strawberries with water. Then take off the leaves.
3. Put the banana, strawberries, milk, and ice cream into the blender.
4. Have an adult help you mix everything together until smooth.
5. Pour your shake into a glass. Enjoy!

peel to take the skin off a piece of fruit

ripe when fruits are fully grown and ready to eat; ripe fruits taste best

vines long, thin plants that look like ropes; vines grow on trees and fences

vitamins things in food that keep your body healthy and growing

Read More

Maestro, Betsy C. *How Do Apples Grow*? New York: HarperCollins Children's Books, 1993.

Pickering, Robin. *I Like Oranges*. New York: Scholastic Library Publishing, 2000.

Rockwell, Lizzy. *Good Enough to Eat: A Kid's Guide to Food and Nutrition*. New York: HarperCollins Children's Books, 1999.

Explore the Web

DOLE FIVE A DAY
http://www.dole5aday.com

F&V (FRUITS & VEGETABLES) FOR ME
http://www.fandvforme.com.au

THE PRODUCE PATCH
http://www.aboutproduce.com/producepatch

Ripe plums are sweet and juicy.